Usborne First Stories

SLEEPING BEAUTY

Retold by Heather Amery
Illustrated by Stephen Cartwright

Language Consultant: Betty Root
Reading and Language Information Centre
University of Reading, England

There is a little yellow duck to find on every page.

Once upon a time, there lived a King and a Queen.
They were always very sad because they had no
children. At long last after waiting many years, a
baby daughter was born. The King and Queen
were delighted and loved the little Princess.

When the baby Princess was christened, the King and Queen gave a great feast at the Palace. Six good fairies came but the King had forgotten to invite the wicked, bad-tempered fairy whom no one had seen for years. She was very angry.

After the feast, the good fairies made special wishes for the baby. When she grew up, they wanted her to be good, beautiful, clever and to sing and dance. The sixth good fairy was just about to make her wish when the wicked fairy appeared, looking cross.

"This is my wish for the Princess," she said. "When she is seventeen, she will prick her finger on a spinning wheel. Then she will die."

"Oh, no," cried the sixth fairy. "My wish is that she won't die but will sleep for a hundred years."

The King shouted and the Queen cried but the wicked fairy disappeared in a puff of smoke. "Well," said the King. "I'll make a new law. All spinning wheels in my kingdom must be burned. Then the Princess can't prick her finger."

As the years passed and the Princess grew up, she became good, beautiful and clever, and could sing and dance. On her seventeenth birthday, there was a Grand Ball at the Palace and the six good fairies came. Everyone had forgotten the wicked fairy.

The next day, the Princess found a little staircase in the Palace she had never seen before.

She pushed open the door and saw an old woman with a spinning wheel. "Come in, my dear," said the old woman, who was really the wicked fairy.

"What are you doing?" asked the Princess, who had never seen a spinning wheel. "I'm spinning," said the old woman. "I'll show you how to do it. Come and hold this." The princess put out her hand. "Oh," she said, "I've pricked my finger."

In a second, the Princess was fast asleep.
Downstairs the King yawned, the Queen yawned
and everyone else yawned. Then they went to sleep.

The six good fairies carried the sleeping Princess to
her bedroom and laid her on her bed.

In the Palace, nothing, not even a mouse, moved for a hundred years. Outside, a thick forest grew up all round it until only the roof showed above tree tops. No one went near it but the good fairies watched over it while everyone and everything slept.

After exactly one hundred years, a young Prince went hunting near the Palace. He saw the roof above the trees and asked an old man about it. "My grandfather told me it's enchanted and there's a beautiful princess asleep in it," said the old man.

The Prince thanked the old man and walked towards the forest round the Palace. When he reached it, the trees parted and let him through.

He ran up the Palace steps, past the sleeping guards. It was so quiet, it was rather creepy.

He searched the whole palace and, at last, came to
the Princess's bedroom. When he saw her lying
asleep, he thought she was so beautiful, he bent
over and kissed her. The Princess opened her eyes
and smiled. "You have come at last," she said.

All over the palace, everyone woke up, yawned, stretched, shook off the dust and started to move about. "I'm hungry," said the King. "Tonight we'll have a feast." He thanked the Prince for coming to their rescue and the Queen invited him to stay.

Next day, the Prince asked the King if he could marry the Princess. "Of course," said the King and the Princess said, "Yes, please." There was a grand wedding and the six good fairies were invited. And the Prince and Princess lived happily ever after.

First published in 1988. Usborne Publishing Ltd, 20 Garrick Street, London WC2E 9BJ. © Usborne Publishing Ltd. 1988